# LITTLE JORDAN

# LITTLE JORDAN

A NOVEL BY

*Marly Youmans*

DAVID R. GODINE, *Publisher*
BOSTON · MASSACHUSETTS

David R. Godine, *Publisher*
P.O. Box 9103
Lincoln, Massachusetts 01773

ACKNOWLEDGMENTS
Special thanks is due to the New York Foundation for
the Arts for a 1991-1992 Fellowship in fiction.
The opening chapter of *Little Jordan* appeared in the
Winter 1995 issue of *The Carolina Quarterly*.

Library of Congress Cataloging-in-Publication Data
Youmans, Marly.
Little Jordan : novel / by Marly Youmans. —1st ed.
p.  cm.
ISBN 1-56792-029-2
I. Title.
PS3575.068L58  1995  813´:54—DC20  95-17092
CIP

*First edition*
Printed in the United States of America

*For Michael*

# One ⌇

THE GHOST figures, drifting and catching on last year's corn stalks and dry teasel, told us the summer ahead would be a strange one. And it was: a summer that came to mean white shapes floating on Little Jordan creek; a summer my momma fell—fell like a dropped stone—in love with a man too like Hinton, my daddy; a summer when I kissed my first boy and when I learned that sad things can come and come and not break us, even when we want to be broken. Most of us, anyhow, can't be broken that way. *The Summer of Isidore*, I call it, though Momma still says that Isidore is no right name for a woman. As if all Isidore's troubles might have come from being named wrong, when anybody can see what happened was only the bad luck of a screen door.

They were ghost figures. That's what it seemed to me with twilight sinking into our big yard of walnut trees. It gets blue under the trees while Mr. Massey's fields are brightening in the tail end of the sun. So when I saw those sunlit people, wandering through a fallow field, pushing some of last year's stalks aside, I couldn't think what they were, what they could be doing. Our yard, which Fred Massey mows with a tractor, runs down to the dirt road and the creek, and pretty soon I caught white glimpses of people starting and stopping along Little Jordan, wading the stream. Sifting into the edges of our yard.

Maybe it was just because I was thirteen and fresh out of school for summer and expecting something—trouble or a meeting or just something new—but I darted from window to window, sure that *something* had begun. The figures glistened under the walnut trees, and lights rocked on the water. I locked the front door and looked out the fisheye peephole. In its shiny globe, all figures turned toward our door.

"Momma!" I called. "Momma, come here quick."

bouncing with excitement. Her bare
...hind me, but I didn't unglue myself

Momma peeked out the curtains.

ghosts," I said.

...e stared out the window.

"It's those people from the other side of Little Jordan, on top of the slope," she said. "Don't know what they're doing."

Momma has always been a woman of action.

"Excuse me," she said, doling out a smile, and opened the door.

I hovered there at the window, looking at Momma talking to a couple of men.

After a while I plucked up my courage and slipped out on the porch where I could see better. Momma was asking questions. I could hardly pick out her figure in the dark, except for her bare feet. Momma's feet are shaped just like fans, from too much going barefoot, and they gleamed in the grass. She looked even smaller than usual, especially standing next to those two men. I thought that one of them might be a sheriff or deputy, and the other I recognized as someone who walke[d] hunting dogs down our dirt road. A group of peo[ple] moved across the lawn, lightly beating the overgrow[n] fence dividing our yard from the fields. Some of them had already disappeared into the pasture behind our house, while others were walking back and forth along the creek.

I sighed with disappointment. Things were taking on an everyday look.

But there was something: a woman swaying beside the green and luminous clusters of a snowball bush. From the porch steps I could see her eyes, large and black. She held her hands to her face, as if she were looking in them, as though her hands were a mirror. She wore a white sundress that swept below her knees. Bending toward the glowing tree, she was nothing so much as a moth feeding upon a flower.

I stared at the woman until someone came and led her back toward the ridge. They should have left her there, swaying all night against that snowhill of flowers.

Those were my first thoughts about Isidore, before I heard her name, before I spoke to her or touched her hand. Isidore's summer had started out in the twilight, under the walnut trees.

\*

Momma was subdued by the time she came back to the porch.

"Did you see the woman in white?"

I nodded.

"They're looking for her little girl," she said.

Momma told me what she had heard; that while Isidore napped after dinner, her three year-old daughter must have climbed out of her crib and pushed the screen door as far as it would go and squeezed herself outside. A neighbor glimpsed a child who clapped her hands and vanished between trees, but since then, nothing.

"It's a sad thing," Momma said. She twisted my hair into a stubby ponytail, and I let her pull my head toward her.

"What would I have done all these years without my little horror?"

"Little horror," I repeated, thinking of the woman like a white moth.

Momma teases me all the time. Even when she doesn't feel like joking, she jokes. It's a habit.

"Don't be sad," she whispered, hugging me. "They'll find her. A baby like that can't go far."

In the creek and fields, more of the long oval beams of flashlights switched on. A few lanterns made unsteady circles across the lawn. Now we could hear the searchers calling the child's name, a three-noted song repeated endlessly.

"Will they go on like that all night?" I asked.

"If they have to," Momma said. "The poor mother."

"She's so beautiful."

"Mmm."

"Couldn't we help look?"

"Tomorrow, if they haven't found her, we'll look," Momma promised.

Still, it was hard just to go inside and lock the door, so we moved out into the yard. We wandered under the walnut trees for a while, pretending we weren't searching for the baby. A few wavering fireflies rose from the ground, but they weren't enough light to see by. Under the trees we heard the child's name called from farther downstream, the sound half-buried under the noise of water, pouring and pouring eastward.

Some of the lights receded to the far meadows. From our distance, searchlights shone no brighter than the fireflies.

"They'll find her," Momma said.

That wasn't the way it happened, though. It's easy to lose things, hard to find them. So many times I've circled through our five rooms, looking for a book or a glass, and ended by forgetting what I was searching for in the first place. A called child might hide, might run from strange voices: even familiar voices can sound eerie in the woods or fields.

They didn't find her. None of those men and women working back and forth along the stream with their lamps and lights found her.

That night I dreamed of a white moth, seesawing on the verge of an immense blossom. Three notes spiraled free from the flower's heart and spilled onto the breeze. And when I woke in the morning, I found the lost child.

*

It's the people who don't really look who find things most often. And I wasn't looking, at least not for her; I was just looking at the early morning, which had forgotten all about lost children and was busy drenching every chink between the leaves with sun. The three-noted song had flown upstream and to the ridge. Frogs shrilled a summer's sound that made me think of nothing but being home from school for three long months. I raced through the noise of insects, down to the creek. A mass of jewelweed had sprung up around the banks, and its green foam broke against my legs, flecking them with leaves and curled snails. Ice water so mountain-cold it numbed my legs flashed a chill up my spine. My feet remembered the slick stones that paved the streamside and the secret path of submerged rocks to the other shore. I dashed across, then back again.

Balancing with arms out on an up-tilted rock, I saw her: saw something cold as the stream. What I glimpsed first was floating whiteness, cloth knotted around a stick under the water. More like a reflection than anything else, so that I glanced up; nothing but stems and leaves between stream and sun. The air felt colder. There was a quiet moment between seeing a thing like the reflection of a cloud and knowing. The previous night, the song, and my dream flooded in. Still, I wasn't sure. This is part of what I have learned: some things have to be grasped with the hands to be believed. But back then I didn't think. I had stopped all thinking except whatever urge made me wade farther and farther into the rush of the stream, so that I swayed and light jostled before my eyes. Then my hand reached out like an alien thing. Someone else's hand, or not an arm and hand at all—a white snake, a peeled sapling in the wind. There; it was done. The rotten branch cracked and the pale shape swung free, dipping under the water and rising, threatening to roll over on the current. I couldn't have that; I couldn't bear to see it roll over in the stream. I wanted to keep the thing quiet. I was afraid to touch it, but more than that I was afraid of the stream's tumble, afraid to see the shape changed or be revealed. So I groped for the whiteness.

She was not a baby. She was not a baby at all. Until then, I had not realized that a three year-old was so large. Her leg felt heavy in my hand, heavy and slippery with water. I towed her through the deep places, keeping my eyes fastened on the white blur of her body. I gasped with the cold.

When I came to the shallows, I stopped, afraid of seeing her face at last and afraid of hurting her, dragging her over the stones. Tears kept getting on my face. Gripping the other leg, I hoisted her, dank and weightier than anything I had ever lifted, into the air. The child's head bounced against my legs and swung outward. Clumsily I laid her on the ground beside the stream, face down. I couldn't think. I couldn't think what to do. The earth was damp and crawling with small bugs and snails. I looked toward the house: it had never seemed so far from Little Jordan. Too far to call. I didn't want to leave the child alone. I don't know why that seemed so important then, as though something else might happen to her.

Finally I stripped off my nightgown and spread it on a patch of grass, then stood shivering in my panties. I made myself go over to the child and pull her up by the arms, the way you grasp hold of a boy or girl when you're playing 'statues,' then let her down with a thud. It took me a minute to look at her, but when I did I saw that she appeared small, lying on my nightgown. Her eyes were shut, her mouth barely open, so that the teeth showed. Maybe the shadows under the trees did it, or maybe the coldness of the stream, but she was blue all over, from her face to the stiff legs. She looked a little puffy, too, although I could see that she might once have been pretty. A pretty child. I felt relieved that there were no leeches. When I finished looking at her, I straightened her clothes and carried water in my cupped hands to wash leaves and hair from her face. It didn't take long.

From the stream our house looked small as a playhouse, and the big grove of walnuts blocked the light. There was no way to reach the house and watch the child at the same time. I stood with my arms wrapped around my chest, covering the pink puckers that were all I had of breasts. I wasn't crying anymore. I felt quiet.

"Momma," I called, so softly that no one would ever hear. Then I called again and again, until I couldn't stop calling and I was crying again, my voice rasping out of me louder than any voice I had ever heard.

Momma, momma, momma: my cries filled the walnut grove, widening like circles in a pond until the far-off door flew open and Momma came running to where I stood, my arms out, legs littered with snails and stems, Isidore's new-washed child lying with clenched eyes and a faint, open smile at my feet.

# Two ஐ

Much later, when my nightgown was returned, I examined it closely. The fabric smelled of violets, and someone had ironed it, a thing that was never done in our house. That evening while Momma showered I pulled it on. The gown gave me a ghostly feeling, as though Isidore's child lingered in its folds. When I looked at myself in the mirror, my nightgown seemed more present than I did.

I carefully folded the gown and put it away at the back of a dresser drawer. After that, the smell of violets clung to my other nightgowns, and eventually all my folded clothes took on sweetness.

Violets. June was covered over with flowers, in yards

and fields and at Morgan's Funeral Home where Momma and I waited in line with the ridge people and family friends. By then we knew Isidore's name and had learned that she was pregnant, that she was married to a man named Bill Simms who worked as a physician's assistant at the town hospital. I shook his hand hard, because Momma says no one admires a hand like a sick fish, and was introduced to his parents, and hers. Isidore sat with a woman who might have been her sister. You couldn't catch Isidore's attention; her eyes kept sliding over faces, even when they spoke to her. The other woman would answer, nodding and pressing people's hands.

Flowers were jammed in ranks behind and beside the coffin, which didn't resemble any coffin I ever saw—more like an iced cake. The lid was sealed tight, and I wondered whether the little girl was still blue, or whether she had turned pink when she warmed up. On top perched a saddle of ferns and roses, tiny ones without any smell. When we walked past I touched the coffin with my fingertips. It felt cold. Even though Momma says that spiritual life is a myth, I said a 'Dear God, if you're there, please' sort of prayer.

As we left, the line of visitors snaked down the street. On the porch kids swung and rocked in green metal furniture. The grown-ups told them *hush*, but it only takes a couple of loudmouths to make a good noise.

That summer another set of flowers—other than the ones popping and bursting around us—caught our attention. These came sailing like flower boats on Little Jordan, riding the riffles, swooping up and down on the waves. From Mr. Massey's one-at-a-time-at-your-own-risk suspension bridge to the quiet pools, I found them moored on leaves, over-turned and drowning, tearing pell-mell downstream to the Lark River and then maybe even past Grandma and Grandpa's house beside the sea. I never saw one that wasn't white, and I never saw who floated them down our stream. I imagined Isidore kneeling on the bank, launching the flowers in the shallows. Or ridge kids even, robbing gardens and toppling the blooms off the edge of Massey's swinging bridge, watching them sink and bob back to the surface, then teeter off down the creek.

The shut coffin, the smell of violets, the traveling flowers: it was a summer of secrets. When I saw my friends, I couldn't talk about the child I had hauled from the stream. This single act was the most serious thing that had ever happened to me. It was a secret thing, a white blur buried in water, but every day in the fields or on the big lawn, it floated up and spun my thoughts toward death. And although I skipped from stone to stone, following the flower boats, I never swam in the stream again.

\*

Days idled by, no different from the days of other summers. *Languid*, Momma said. They dipped and slid like a petal that makes its run down Little Jordan and never meets worse than a stone in its journey, that lightly twirls away from twigs and leaves.

Under the walnut trees the leafy dark grew denser. Black and white mushrooms, shiny and bold, reared up in the gloom. The bundle of hibiscus sticks beside my window broke into leaves and flowered, spilling ruffles from the top. Powdery stamens floated free from blooms stained violet at the heart. Wrung blossoms littered the yard. Every detail was exactly as it had appeared the summer before, so that every bend and slant of grass seemed remembered.

Even the creek flowed on with its familiar sounds, and although I imagined some withheld secret deep in its chilly pools, I could see nothing new there. But I remember that I felt sure down to the marrow that things had changed. Grandma—that's my Grandma Lyons, not Hinton—calls the time after something big happens "waiting for the next shoe to drop." I asked her what it meant once; she smiled and never answered me, and I'd still like to know. Shoes. Maybe I was waiting for the next shoe that summer.

It seems that the next shoe doesn't fall until you've given up expecting it to drop. Momma was shut in the house, sweating over Fall lesson plans for her new eleventh-grade honors class in History. I wasn't doing much of anything, sprawled across our big hammock reading a book. So at first, I didn't notice a woman walking up the dirt road from the direction of Massey's bridge.

When I spotted her, she was poised above the creek pools. I rolled over on my side and peered through the mesh. A bobwhite with a waggly tail of little ones came peeping out of a hedgerow, and the woman whirled and stared straight at me—though I didn't know if she actually saw me under the fir tree. *Isidore.* She edged along the margin of the stream, pushing through vines and jewelweed, her white dress trailing through soaked leaves. Plenty of times in the past few weeks I too had scouted along the creek, examining the water's edge and the pools, so dark that you could imagine anything. For a moment she stood on a tablestone at the edge of the big pool, and I could see her standing on tiptoe, lifting her dress out from her sides like wings.

Then she crashed from sight, her arms outspread and her body as straight as a felled tree. I churned in the hammock, which struggled against me, spinning me up tight, then unspinning until I hit the ground.

I sped over to Momma's bedroom window and pressed my face against the screen. She was in there, hunched and dark and mumbling.

"Momma!" I shouted, making her jump. "Momma, she's in the creek. Come quick!"

Momma popped out the front door, fussing at me and starting for the water at the same time. She darted out of the house like a cuckoo springing out of a Swiss clock.

"It's her," I panted, running and holding my side where the hammock had dumped me on a hard root. "It's her."

Momma flapped behind me, calling *Who? Who?* and later on she said that she had a scary feeling that we'd find the little girl all over again.

Flying out from under the walnuts' big umbrellas of shade, I caught sight of Isidore plunging back under the stream.

Momma and I raced past the trees and road and into the weeds, hardly stopping until we stumbled knee-deep in Little Jordan. For a split second we stared down at the hair drifting black on black water and at the white dress before we both grabbed for whatever we could reach, hoisting her up by shoulders and hair and dress. Ice-cold water sluiced from her back; she gasped as water trickled from her open mouth. Momma and I held her up between us, and I saw again that Isidore was beautiful. As beautiful as the serious angels on cards tucked in Grandma Lyons' family Bible.

We scraped her knees dragging her out of the creek,

and Momma knelt to look at the cut, which began to bleed slowly.

"What did you think you were doing?" Momma asked. "What did you think?"

Isidore didn't answer but let us walk her toward the house. Under the walnut trees she began shaking with cold. When she stopped and looked back at the stream, we waited.

"Isidore," Momma said. "Isidore."

Drooping a little, she allowed herself to be pushed forward. In the house Momma turned on the shower and let the hot water run until the bathroom grew steamy. I stared, then looked away; I had never seen anything like Isidore's milky breasts blue with veins and her long pregnant belly, tight and round at the base.

"You should think of the baby," Momma said. "You've got to take care of yourself. Think of this baby."

Momma made her words clear and slow, as though Isidore herself were a baby.

Afterward Momma helped Isidore into a terry robe, then bandaged the cut on her knee. She sent me outside with Isidore's clothes, which I clipped to the line and pulled taut, so they would dry without too many wrinkles.

Momma and Isidore murmured in the living room. I leaned on the screen door and looked in, and Momma looked back at me for a moment and smiled. I could've gone inside, but I sat down in the sunshine where I could hear their voices rise and fall. The grass prickled against my damp legs. I wanted the afternoon to be over so that Momma and I could talk. I could hardly think of anything except Isidore's body, swollen and strange. So that was it, that was part of being a woman.

The noon sun ladled its heat over the house, the rocking voices, the grass. I went on thinking and thinking until Isidore became a part of the sound of the stream, the heat of the ground. When I woke she was gone, and Momma sat beside me on the lawn.

I laid my head in Momma's lap, something I hadn't done in a long, long time, and she stroked my hair.

# *Three* ⁓

THE WEATHER turned hot, hot as the dog days. Things were getting on my nerves. I put it down to the heat and the insect whine that already had scaled to the level of an August noon. In the field closest to our house, Fred Massey was putting up a tent. I watched him from my hammock. It took him just about all morning, but I didn't offer to help, even though I knew how to manage a tent better than that. It was a dome tent, and he kept getting the support poles stuck halfway through their casings. Afterward, he traveled about a good bit. He'd vanish into the tent, come back out and look around, then move it again. I figured he was testing the ground for lumps and rocks. I could have told him that he'd chosen a pretty lousy spot. In the first place, the middle of a field is warm. And a hay field isn't the best choice either. Fred Massey had mown it himself a week before, so you'd think he would have known better. The surface was coarse and stubbly after the early cutting, and in our dry hot June the new growth hadn't forced the fresh stems through the old yet. There was a good spot for camping down near the stream. Years back Fred Massey's father had rolled a lawn for tennis—back when he and Mrs. Massey were newlyweds and lived in our house. I can't imagine Mr. Massey playing tennis. The lawn is partly tangled with blackberry canes, but in the center the grass grows smooth and green. I figured Fred's dad didn't tell him about the place.

Finally Fred let the tent rest. He dived through the doorway, then re-emerged. Right away, he found out that it's fairly hot in a dark green tent. My watch said two o'clock. Fred sat cross-legged in front of the tent and didn't move.

The minute hand crawled to half past and he still hadn't stirred.

In our valley the warmth swarms across your back on

a really hot day. Pinpoints of heat explode against your skin. Before I made it across the yard, my back felt soaked. Crushing the stubs of dry grass, I lumbered over to the tent, loud as could be. Trying to step quietly all the while. Not that anyone could sneak up on Fred Massey.

He didn't look up, just sat looking at a couple of ants that were making a puzzled trek around and around his leg.

"What are you doing?" I asked. I had to ask twice.

"I was having trouble with the fifth," he said.

I invited myself to sit down on the grass in front of him. "Thank you, don't mind if I do," I said, crossing my legs neatly. Scratchy ground, just as I thought.

"The fifth?" I asked. Sometimes you have to prompt Fred Massey. He thinks a lot. He gets distracted.

"Uh-huh," he said.

"The fifth . . ." I repeated, drawing the word out.

Fred looked up. He was fifteen, good-looking, strong from farm work. He had the sort of intent expression on his face that makes people say that somebody's eyebrows are drawn together. Honestly, my stomach dropped an inch or two when I met his blue eyes. Not that I stood alone in that kind of behavior. Half the girls in our school had crushes on Fred Massey.

"Fifth commandment," he said.

I was so busy with that fluttery feeling in my stomach and with trying not to sweat that I almost forgot my question.

"Oh," I said.

"It's getting pretty hard to work with that one," he explained, stabbing at some more ants in the grass. "I thought maybe it would be a little easier out here."

"Fred," I said, "it's just slipped my mind—which one is the fifth?"

He lay back in the grass and shielded his eyes with his arm. I hoped he wouldn't guess right off that I couldn't tell five from ten, although I did know about the burning bush and Moses. I pictured him coming down from a mountain, beard electrical, stones in his hands.

"Honor thy father and mother," he said.

"Oh." I hadn't met up with that one before. It sounded like a fine idea. I honored Momma a good bit, but I couldn't imagine honoring Hinton, even if it was a fine idea.

"I can see how it would be easier from down here," I

said. "The honoring, I mean." He had come about as far from the front door of his house as he could get and still raise his tent on legal Massey dirt. Any farther and he would be off Mr. Massey's lower fields and onto our rented yard. Which was also Mr. Massey's land, strictly speaking.

Fred cast out a suspicious glance, like he thought maybe I was trying to be sarcastic. I wasn't though. I had a lot of respect for Fred.

I shifted slightly. Lying at full-length in that tent would be as bad as curling up on a bed of nails. And hot.

"How about some lemonade?"

That worked on him right away. You could just see him getting thirsty, thinking about a big frosted glass of ice and lemons. When I stood up, I could see a car parked in the lane. My mother's latest boyfriend.

"Look, I'll run get the lemonade," I said. "We'll drink it over here, at your house."

I could tell he was pleased about that "your house" business. Like a little kid, I thought, dragging a sheet over some chairs and pretending a tent was home. Moving out on his momma.

After a week I gave in and told Fred Massey about the old tennis lawn, then helped him move the tent down to the stream. It staked in easy, the ground soft and black by the water. The seams leaked a few slow tears every hour, but the lawn was perfect compared to the field. Momma told Fred that he could come and use our "facilities," and he did drop by to talk and drink our lemonade a few times. Mostly, I was the one who stopped by his tent-house. It fronted the dirt lane, so we could hardly avoid saying "hello" at least. Sometimes in the day I would catch glimpses of him working in the upper fields with his father. Evenings he would unwind in his blackberry-walled yard. After dinner Fred and I often talked out on the tennis lawn, and though at first I was nervous, it didn't take long until I felt pretty comfortable with him. At night I would lie in bed, sleepless, thinking about the child in the stream, remembering Fred Massey's profile that looked like the face of a king on a gold coin in one of Momma's history books.

He was the only one I ever told about Isidore, about her daughter.

"Most kids would have been afraid to touch her," he said. "Why didn't you want to talk about it?"

Fred lay stretched out in the damp grass, looking off toward the Massey farmhouse, where lights burned in the dusk.

"Because it's mine," I said. Mine. A secret, a whiteness in black water. To be read, known. Or kept as mystery.

I did tell him a lot about Isidore, though. That June, I had fallen half in love with Isidore and half with Fred Massey. I told Fred how Momma and I walked to Isidore's every day or so, just to check. How we liked her—liked her quiet and even her sadness, her candor, and how glad she was to see us, never holding it against me that I had found her child. How we never told her husband, Bill Simms, anything about the stream, about how she toppled in on purpose and lay there drinking in the creek, her hair spread out on the black water.

"Why didn't you tell him—why didn't your mother tell him?" Fred asked, rolling closer so he could inspect my answer.

I could smell Fred Massey's sweaty skin, mingled with a sweet odor of hay.

"Because." I paused, looking in his eyes, then glanced to his shoulder and muscular arm, then to the stream, to the farmhouse moored on a distant hillside.

"Why?"

I thought about why—it wasn't just that we felt she was fated to be our friend and that in return we owed her silence and loyalty—or that we wouldn't tell tales.

"I didn't feel sure," I said slowly.

"Sure of what?"

"Sure that leaping into Little Jordan was strange. It didn't seem so strange to me. I could picture her needing to know how cold the water was. Needing to look underneath."

He didn't reply.

"I don't know," I said. "I might have done the same thing. Might have wanted to feel it—water, something. Find out what things meant, feel what my daughter had felt. Feel the water hugging me—instead of a baby."

My face was warm. I had said too much. But what had happened, what was there to know? Was Momma right, that Isidore's little girl would never be seen again, never again?

"You're a strange girl, Meg," Fred said. He sighed, as if he had been holding his breath.

Neither of us said a word for a long time.

"I guess I'll go home some day soon," he said, sitting up.

"Because I'm strange?" I felt sure I would cry, partly because Fred was going home and partly because I didn't keep my mouth shut about Isidore.

"No." Fred laughed then, and he put his arm around my shoulders—touching me for the first time. He gazed up at the hill fields. Two figures inched about on the upper slopes, and I guessed the big one was Fred's father. Fred smiled, watching them. Smiling like the "purest fool," as Grandpa Lyons used to say.

"Yesterday," he said, still looking up at the hills, "my mom told me that running away from one thing just leads you to chase after another."

That gave me a quirk of surprise, and I was busy puzzling over what it meant when Fred leaned closer and rubbed his face against mine. Then he kissed me, not the way I had seen Momma and her boyfriend kiss, working a lot of struggle into it, but very quietly. Quiet as dew.

For a minute I saw his eyelashes against his skin and felt his cheek, cool and smooth like a little boy's cheek.

Maybe all first kisses are the same, or maybe none of them are. Mine started with thinking about a boy's mother, a boy's cheek. Then suddenly everything seemed to change, as though I had stepped into deep water, and I closed my eyes.

*

The dam, only a mile away if we cut through Massey woods, became our goal on the hottest summer afternoons. We could wade upstream until Little Jordan narrowed and sank under a road. Balancing on a sewage pipe clamped to a tunnel wall, we followed. Then up a steep slope snarled in vines. Last came a hike through woods, which ended abruptly at a pebble beach beside the dam.

The far shore of the lake was bleached and bare. Copperheads basked on the rocks, coiling and uncoiling. The stone beach was a snake nest; my skin crawled. The dam was old, and Mama once saw it on a list of our region's ten worst dams. We don't live in such a well-heeled state.

Like the trestle over Lark River or the wild caves at the lake's eastern edge, the dam was sacred ground to Fred Massey. Testing ground. When he flung himself into the air, I saw how much there was of him, tall and big enough to make a dent in the air and just sit there for seconds before gravity took hold. Then nothing—then bubbles, a head shrunk small on the water's surface.

"I touched bottom," he yelled, throwing his head back and gasping.

"Did you see snakes?" I whispered. My fingers clamped like suckers to the dam's stone curb.

"Come on—the water's just right," he called.

I didn't so much leap as give myself up to the air and to the fact that Fred Massey had certificates, framed certificates, on his bedroom wall, one for lifesaving and one for CPR. Limp, shivering, I stepped into air—was thrust down corridors of wind and water—slammed through pale green until my foot touched muck and flinched away. The rising was ever so much more slow than the breathless, baptismal falling, slow enough to see gleams on the ceiling of the lake. I burst through the surface, my head crowned with streaks of sun, my lungs shuddering with air. I could see Fred Massey towering in the noon sun, calling and plunging into air, plummeting past, touching me in the water so that I jumped as though a young snake had brushed his scales against me. I trembled and flung drops from my fingertips.

# Four ‿

THE CORN reached to my shoulder, and beautiful ribbons of it clung to our sleeves. Stinging saddleback caterpillars might lurk underneath or above a blade, so I kept my arms pressed close to my sides as I dodged among the heavy stalks, trailing Fred Massey to his secret hiding place. Arching back and forth in the corn made me think of past summers. From as far back as I can remember, Mr. Massey has always brought Momma and me bushels of corn. When I was small, I loved to play in the fresh shucks and tassels while Momma husked the corn. Every bushel hid at least one corn doll, cinched to an ear of corn. They were the same small prizes of summer that Grandma Lyons had given Momma when she was a girl—tiny cobs swaddled in delicate husks. When Momma peeled away the shucks, crinkled silks appeared, the ripply and tender green hair of the corn doll. The miniature cob shone, each kernel smaller than a baby's tooth.

I lost sight of Fred.

Dreamily I zigzagged through the field. I imagined the thousands of corn plants on the Massey farm, imagined thousands more in green belts around the world. Some would have ears smaller than corn dolls; some would be already ripening.

Years back, Momma told me that the dolls were the Corn Woman's papooses, snuggled next to the corn. She showed me the Woman's corn milk, beading up on the kernels. And once she said that the dolls were the tears of the Corn Woman. As if a woman's grief and children might be one. I now knew they could be the same, in a way—just as surely as if I had pulled Isidore's daughter from a stream of tears.

Long ago, Grandma Lyons told these stories to her little girl. Though Momma believes in common sense, she still likes to tell about the Corn Woman.

*

We forded Little Jordan at the eastern edge of the Massey farm, where deep water muscled past stone ledges and plunged away in rapids. Fred Massey grabbed my arm as the stream tumbled under my feet, pushing me sideways. Until then, I hadn't known our creek could be so strong, and for one flashing instant I pictured myself as a white blur under the swirling water.

Clambering up the rocks, I scraped my knees.

"Just like a kid," Fred said, but he didn't mind. I lay on my back, breathing heavily through my nose— trying not to sound winded. Fred was talking but I couldn't listen. My knees stung, and the blood on them slowly dried in the heat, turning stiff and shiny.

My breath relaxed, grew regular.

"This is your secret place?"

Fred rolled over on his side and stared at me. His wet hair looked slick and jet black.

"Your eyes are really, really blue," I said.

"You weren't listening. Come on," Fred said, standing and offering to pull me up. For a boy, he had strong arms. Momma told me there was nothing like baling hay to give a person strength.

Circled by trees, Fred Massey's hiding place lay within earshot of the water. Noise bounced on leaves and slopes; the stream seemed to bubble over our heads.

"These foundations are from the old Black Horse Tavern," Fred said. I expect he had told about the spot once while I lay collapsed on the grass, but he told it over again and I didn't complain.

We wandered through the stone foundations. Cushions of star moss and mats of short, fine grass dotted the ground where rooms once stood.

"There's the front entrance of the tavern. The cookhouse in back."

Fred pointed out six stone circles. "The innkeepers piled rocks around apple trees to protect them from animals."

One broken-down tree still sheltered inside a ring of stones. Remains of a garden, lily-of-the-valley beds glistened here and there under the forest trees. A faint track showed, ghost of a trail first tramped by the Cherokee.

"I've been coming here since I was eight," he said. "Nobody else has been here in all those years. Not that I know about."

He easily threaded a path through the shadowy ruins. "Through here," he called, vanishing into darkness.

So the tavern wasn't the secret place. I strayed deeper into the shade, where only scattered beams of light filtered down to the forest floor. Then Fred Massey's arm reached from a hedge and snatched me through. The small old branches snapped and jumped, peppering me with bark and leaves. Bent over, back first, I was towed into Fred Massey's secret room.

He steadied me as I leaned back to see a branching roof that sparkled like the scales of a fish, the bright openings between leaves schooling in one direction, then another; darting and swerving under a breeze as high as the treetops.

"So this is your place," I said.

In the square of shrubbery a drowned light glimmered. By its muted shine I saw a pool of thick black ink, with one or two oval leaves floating on the surface. Moss lapped the coping where a child of stone poured invisible water from an empty jar.

I knelt on the ground, star moss cool against my scraped knees.

"It's beautiful," I said, very softly.

The child must have been chipped from rare marble, because she shone even in that dim light.

"It's like a shrine," I said.

It seemed like a temple of the corn doll's child, to children in a stream of tears. Its mystery—the black water like a solid, the jar emptied but still pouring—gave nothing back. Like my images of Isidore's daughter, her mouth open but not for breath or to tell me a single word, it kept a kind of friendship, a faith, with silence.

One gossamer seed whirled downward and caught on the black pool.

I imagined Fred Massey as a little boy, flung down on stars, falling asleep under the stone girl's gaze. It wasn't hard to do. I had known him my whole life, though I hadn't been looking closely until now.

He put his arm around me, rubbed his cheek against mine, then gave me a small, formal kiss.

\*

By the time I reached my thirteenth birthday, I hadn't called my father 'Dad' in years. Just *Hinton*. Hinton was "feckless" and a "general admirer of women." Hinton abandoned me and Momma for another woman when I turned seven. The afternoon before he left, I remember Momma pacing and crying. When he eventually came home, the back seat of the car was sprinkled with dried leaves. Momma says that I crumpled those leaves until they fell to powder.

If Hinton jerked his arm or tossed back his hair, he seemed to shake down light, his movement was so quick and sharp. In the mornings he dashed out of the house. A fresh-rolled cigarette jutted from his bottom lip, and an acrid smell permeated his clothes. I didn't mind that much. It was when he drank that I feared him—not that he ever hit either of us, although one day he smashed the dining room chairs to tinder and ruined a tiny metal table that had belonged to Momma's grandmother.

Sometimes I hated Hinton.

Momma said that I shouldn't hate him, that I should respect the best qualities in him and forget the rest.

Nobody forced me to remember him, but I did. He lived so far from us that he surely couldn't matter. Yet he did. He lived in Mexico City, where he taught English and "the culture of the United States." By the summer after my thirteenth birthday, he had divorced three wives. And he had another daughter. Her mother was an Indian woman—a Mexican Indian woman—but he never married her. I guess that he saw his other daughter, since she was living in Mexico City.

He didn't remember my birthday—probably didn't even know when it was. In May I got a postcard from him. It was exotic, gaudy with stamps and foreign place names. The photo showed a jumble of ancient pitted gods, heaped up like forgotten lumber. The date was missing, the message brief and jotted down like a telegram—*Hola Meg many profuse apologies for missing your day have thought of marvelous present which will send —H.*

I used it for a bookmark all summer. As a reminder.

The card arrived the day of the annual Historical Society Picnic, one of Momma's favorite days in the year. I usually look forward to the spring picnic because it means that another year of school is almost over. It's always held at the County museum, which is nothing but the old Abbott farmhouse. It's an adzed log house with ripply windows and a dogwood rail corkscrewing up the stairs into a loft. Momma helped collect the exhibits—she's the one who bought the loom and a cannonball bed tied with ropes that she traced to the Abbott family.

That May, I didn't much care for the picnic.

Momma met Len Jarrett after he weaseled into the party as Maggie Simmons' date—not that lack of an invitation would have stopped him. Later on, Momma apologized to Maggie, who served as secretary that year. Momma was acting president, mainly on the strength of teaching history at the school. Maggie Simmons said that it hadn't been a date, that she had just given him a ride. Momma was pleased; she said that she knew Len wouldn't deliberately hurt anyone's feelings.

Ha, I said privately.

Sometimes, Momma thinks what she wants to think.

Before I met Len Jarrett I had overheard Maggie Simmons explain three times that the two of them weren't together. It was something that she must have felt compelled to do. Eventually she even got around to explaining the details to me, but only after I met him and decided that she and we would be better off without him. When grown-ups start explaining to kids, you know something's wrong. Len flitted from group to group, introducing himself. He was a moth out to inspect a bouquet of pastel dresses. Maggie Simmons kept drinking punch, growing wider and higher and casting a bigger shadow on the punch table. As though she might burst suddenly and fling punch tears everywhere. Not that Len had forgotten her entirely; every now and then he would toss a smile and wave in her direction.

Once he had spotted Momma, Len Jarrett changed his route. I was busy serving punch and trying not to splash the tablecloth, but I could see him winding around the loaded tables, his eyes fastened on her. It doesn't take much of a brain to figure why he chose Momma. For one thing, she stuck out as the prettiest woman there. Her hair is pale, shimmery and fluid as water. When I think of Momma what comes to mind first is her liveliness. Her hair and hands and whole frame seem to flash and tremble with life. Momma loves nothing more than a crowd, whether it's kids in a classroom or a bunch of local people who've chipped in to support the Abbott House and dust the antique furniture. She had slipped her feet out of her sandals and was standing barefoot in the clipped grass.

Len Jarrett cut into the group of people surrounding her, silencing them for a moment before they broke into laughter. He knew how to amuse an audience. After a few minutes, he led Momma around the back of the house. He hadn't toured the house before, or, for that matter, dug the garden or swept the chimneys or done any useful work. It was almost sundown, the rooms dim and shadowy.

When Len Jarrett and Momma emerged on the front porch, they were both laughing. I didn't like him. She led him to the punch table, and while Maggie Simmons and I observed her, I recognized the shiny look in Momma's eyes. I've lived through a good many of Momma's boyfriends, so I knew that shine and the straight look she was giving him that held his gaze. She liked him, and she thought maybe she liked him a lot.

Momma never calls me anything but Meg, but she said to Len, "I want you to meet my daughter, Margaret."

His eyes went distant for a moment.

"Your daughter," he said. "You have a daughter."

One of the trustees tapped Momma's arm, and she turned away.

I looked him over from top to bottom. His hair appeared carefully disarranged, flicked back from his face to show his sharply cut features. Len Jarrett was lean and angular all over. Even his feet were narrow and pointed.

"I didn't know," he started to explain, running a hand through his hair.

Momma stepped back to the table and I finally spoke.

"How do you do," I said, offering my hand. His felt delicate, so I smiled and gave it my firmest squeeze.

"So nice to meet a good friend of Maggie's," I added.

He stared at me, his mouth agape.

"Momma," I said, sloshing some punch onto the table-cloth, "Would you and Mr. Jarrett care for a cup of punch?"

She was looking at Len Jarrett.

"Call me Len," he said, not looking at me.

"Momma," I said.

"Do you know, Momma," I said, "Maggie Simmons has been telling us all about Len?"

It was the first and the last occasion when I had the jump on Len Jarrett, and it was the start of a summer campaign. By month's end we were mortal enemies.

\*

Every time I opened a book and saw Hinton's post-card, I thought about Hinton and about Len Jarrett, who seemed as careless and untrustworthy as my father. After he started spending too much time at our house, I stayed in the hammock and read almost every afternoon. Usually he ignored me or teased me; only once did he try to talk about my mother.

"Where's your *beau?*" Len jeered. I couldn't decide whether he mocked lots of people or whether this was a style he'd picked out special to talk to me.

I let *The Deerslayer* slide down on my chest.

"I don't have a *beau,*" I said. I gazed up into the fir tree at the spiders in their webs, trying to make my voice cool and poisonous.

Len pushed the hammock back and forth.

"I would appreciate it if you wouldn't do that," I said.

"Do what? Sit down here beside you?" He sat down.

"Rock your boat?" He leaned back.

"That too," I said softly, drawing my legs away from him.

He smiled and flipped twigs of fir at my book.

"I guess you didn't like me being so snug with——" he said.

He lurched forward but caught himself and pretended not to notice my almost successful maneuver to dump him on the dirt. "With Ellen," he continued. "You know, women need——"

I managed to jolt his feet to the ground, and he stood up, stumbling slightly. He raked his hair back from his face with his fingers, lifting his chin to let me know he was irked and to show off his profile.

Len's eye was more icy than mine when he put on his Haughty Mode. That's what Momma called it—being in the Haughty Mode. Momma always assumed that he was teasing, while I never assumed anything of the kind.

"Some day we'll have a talk about the facts of life. I'd enjoy that," he said.

He dodged both book and branch easily, then bent over and brushed some dirt from *The Deerslayer*.

"Next time take better care of your treasures," he said, holding out the book. When I didn't respond, he pitched it into the hammock. Slipping from the pages, Hinton's postcard fluttered to the ground, and his tumbled gods lay staring up at Len Jarrett.

Hot tears stood in my eyes. As Len walked away, I contemplated hurling the book again.

Later that afternoon, Fred Massey dropped down in the hammock as I was reading—right at the part where they bury Hetty in the lake next to her mother.

"You're wet," I said, indignant.

The hooks in the trees strained under his added weight.

He had come straight from the fields, and his sweat dribbled down my face and leg as he hugged me. Then he peeled the smeared card away from one arm. Was it important, he wanted to know. "No," I said, "not important." Momma was in the house, arguing with her latest boyfriend. Hinton was thousands of miles off, too grown up to send me a letter or a real belated birthday card or to call. But I had Momma, my grandparents, school friends, and now Fred and Isidore. "Not important," I repeated.

"Just a little trouble with the fifth."

*

Fred Massey tugged the stone planter from its spot, exposing a brass key nestled in a ring of dampness. Some wood lice immediately began to trundle busily on the step. We had walked the mile from the Massey farm to the church under full sail, carrying the billowing church linens of priests and deacons and acolytes. Fred Massey's mother had washed and ironed those robes every month for the past seventeen years.

It was a dazzling noon. No sky could possibly be a deeper, stronger blue than our summer sky, just as no clouds could be more distinct and bright than our clouds, and no day-moon could press such a white thumbprint over the violet and green mountains.

Fred wrenched the key back and forth in the lock until the teeth caught, and he swung open the big double doors.

I hadn't been to church much, just occasionally with Grandma and Grandpa Lyons.

Inside, the dark had collected in aisles and corners, and shards of color spun like the gold dust that spins in a sunny house window. The air took a minute to settle.

Then I saw a glossy hardwood floor, reflecting stained glass; the narrow fierce slashes of the side windows, red and blue and green and gold in peaked frames; the heavy curved beams with many slender bent boards between them. The roof looked like the inside of a boat flipped upside down by a giant hand.

"Wait here," he said. "I'll put these in the choir room."

I waited alone in the belly under that boat, inside the banded and colored light of the ribs. Up front glimmered a watery, mottled picture of hills and cedars and a splashing stream like Little Jordan. Then a cross that looked as though flung drops of dew had met in the air, almost by accident.

"More water," I thought, remembering the day before, when Isidore had told me that the spirit of God was a waterfall in which you knelt. But didn't she know better? Wasn't she afraid of drowning?

I didn't stir. Minute by minute the main window paled or shone brighter. Birds, deep blue shadows, arrowed back and forth behind the glass.

If you are thirteen and you are left suddenly in a place that is like nothing else you have known—that resembles, if anything, a broken kaleidoscope puzzled back together under an ark—well, there's nothing to do but feel uneasy. One moment I had laughed with Fred Massey; the next I stumbled into a chamber more set apart than Isidore's leafy front porch, than Fred's secret hiding place.

From one corner gleamed a painting, a Madonna who embraced a leggy boy-Christ. In turn, the child gripped a beautiful gold toy, a top, in one hand. An arm encircled a roofless church, packed with dolls. A single flame, struggling against the gloom, guttered in the rack of candle holders below.

"Let's light a candle for the Simmses' daughter."

I flinched. Fred appeared beside me, vanished again. A second candle flared in its red glass cup.

"What does it mean?"

"It's to remember the dead—you say a prayer for the soul."

He knelt on a cushion below the trembling flames, resting his hands together very simply, as though praying for a dead person were a perfectly natural thing to do.

I said one of my "if" prayers then. "If there's a God, if we have souls . . ." I remembered how cold Isidore's daughter felt against my hands.

"If Fred Massey is right and Momma wrong," I thought, "this really is God's house. This overturned boat. And if so, we are the tiny people crowded in the boy-king's hand." I shivered, cool air from the nave flowing over me like a current.

"Come on," Fred called, standing in the wide doorway. Sunlight fanned across the floor. "Let's jump off the dam."

\*

*Bleached*, that's it. Returning from the lake, I always felt as though the thoughts in my head had been washed away. Each time I was weak and diminished all over again, my hair twisted into a limp knot at my neck.

"How's Fred, the church boy?"

Len. I hadn't even noticed Momma and Len Jarrett snuggled up in our hammock. I kept on walking my wobbly legs toward the house.

"Looks more like the dam and hell to me," he called.

"Thank you, Len," I muttered.

Before Len, Momma used to say that there was no lower life than the pun. She smiled, pushing the hammock with one bare foot.

"Meg, I thought you weren't going swimming at the dam any more," she said. She didn't really seem concerned. She didn't seem altogether there. The funny part was that I really wished she would get mad and pronounce the dam off limits.

"Just this once. Fred Massey wanted to go." I stopped and sized up the two of them. I was near enough to linger and be friendly.

"Len made a lime soufflé," she said. "Delicious. But it's all gone now."

She smiled at him, then at me.

"Len's been reciting Longfellow."

"Longfellow?"

"What becomes of *Puk-Wudjies*? Who will care for the *Puk-Wudjies*?" Len declaimed. He put his arms around Momma. I felt pretty *Puk-Wudjie* myself. Why had I come back home? To sit around and wait for Len to leave? I would have to listen to his Longfellow and to his talk about moving in. He brought up the idea almost every day. I couldn't figure whether he wanted to live with Momma or whether he just liked to annoy me.

"I'm going to Isidore's," I said. "I'll be back in a while."

"Okay," Momma said. "Just don't stay too long."

"Baim-wawa!" Len said.

Too much fresh air, I thought.

Momma waved.

"This too will pass," I said, looking just above Len's left shoulder. It was a line one of my teachers liked to say. I noticed that it came in handy for most occasions.

*

I spent many afternoon hours curled in Isidore's porch swing while she sat with her swollen feet propped up on the porch railing. Sometimes Momma and I went together; other times I was alone. I trailed the stream banks west to Mr. Massey's hanging bridge, then climbed the hill and followed a meadow path to the cluster of houses. I never took a short-cut across the creek and up the slope, the path Isidore's daughter must have come.

The white porch had a ceiling painted with the same shade of milky green as all porch ceilings in our region. No different in kind from the others, but the leaves and light and Isidore made this one special. Behind the wisteria vines it was shady and cool, and Isidore's pale dresses cast a further shadow, a ring of quiet. I could sit still and comfortable with her, idly watching the antics of a few gauzy flies or the fluttering patches of light between leaves or the shapes the clouds took.

Isidore never minded when I talked about Len Jarrett and Momma. I didn't talk about Hinton much because I was so busy hating Len.

"Why did she pick him?" I asked.

Isidore spoke slowly, as if considering and testing her replies.

"He's smart. Nice looking. He likes to cook—that's important. Unusual."

"He's not nice," I countered.

"He's not boring either. Ellen says he knows a lot about history. He reads." Isidore was sympathetic but she always reminded me why Momma liked Len Jarrett in the first place. We pored over Len and exhausted him as a topic; as summer sailed on, we talked about my school and whether Isidore should go back to college some day, about Bill Simms and summer and favorite books and what Momma thought about Fred—she liked him—and what I thought about her old boy-friends—not much—and what she thought about God—which I have said already. We talked about Isidore's pregnancy, about what she and Bill would name the baby. There was only one topic that we didn't mention, although not talking seemed to make it a presence, not seen but near: a figure, a blur glimpsed from the corner of an eye.

I decided that Isidore Simms and Fred Massey were good, not goody two-shoes but good in a way I would like to be once I got over hating Hinton, my father.

*

"You've never done it?"

"No, never."

Fred and I lay outstretched in the hiding place, whetting our pocketknives. Mine, steel with a silver haft, belonged to Grandma Lyons when she was a girl.

"I thought it was something boys did." I tested the sharpness of my blade against my thumb.

"Not me," Fred Massey said.

"Anyway," he added, "the guys I know best are Nate and Sam, my cousins. And we're already tied by blood."

"Blood is thicker than water," I murmured.

Fred's big knife came from his father. The blade was nicked and so worn that it looked wavy along the edge.

While our knives flashed on a flat stone lugged from Little Jordan, the marble girl went on sloshing her invisible water into the black pool.

"Sometimes," I said, "water is really thicker than blood."

"Because some people are better to you than one of your own blood relatives?"

"And the water itself—you'd think it would be clear, but it isn't—not this water, not Little Jordan, and not the lake. It's all full of death and snakes and mystery."

I sat up, ready.

"This knife is no good," Fred Massey said, wiping his blade on moss.

"My grandma says Little Jordan is full of sin because

of all the baptisms," he said. "But my mom says it's clean, good to drink."

Rolling over on my back, I slid the blade back in its case, and stared up. Although dusk reigned inside the shrubbery, overhead a jagged patch of morning sky and cloud shone between trees.

"You're going to write me? When I go to the beach?"

"Sure," Fred said. "But don't you write me more than twice. And don't use pink paper or perfume or anything."

"Why would I do that?"

"You never know what people will do," he said, grinding his knife harder.

"Well, I'm not people."

"I know," Fred smiled. "Don't I know."

I ignored him.

"It's ready," I said. "The stone's hot."

Fred opened his hand and I grasped his fingers, feeling the rough calluses and the knot of skin where years back he had punctured his thumb on a strand of barbed wire. Beside his broad palm, Grandma Lyons' pretty knife looked like a toy.

"Punch it right in."

The knife surprised me, piercing the fingertip easily. His blood beaded and wobbled, a perfect globe, then smeared along the blade. First cleaning the knife on a fallen leaf, I snapped it shut.

"Now me."

Mr. Massey's knife pressed uselessly against my skin. Then Fred flicked open the little silver knife and in an instant pricked my finger.

"Sorry. A bit deep," he said.

The sharp ache and the pulse of blood made me feel dizzy.

"It's not so bad—feels like a sting, like a heartbeat." I set my fingertip against his. Blood puddled between our fingers and dribbled onto the moss.

"Now what?" I asked.

"Now nothing," he said. "That's it. Now we're blood-bound. Different from what we were before."

"Different."

"Yes."

Fred Massey's leg was wedged against mine. That felt different, the two of us tangled on the ground, the pained, rapid beat of my finger pressed to his. Blood streaked our arms, joined our palms.

A drop of my blood rolled and tumbled inside Fred Massey, climbing the veins of his forearm, settling for an instant in his heart. I imagined his, in turn, surging through the big and little veins of my body, exploring and alerting the smallest capillaries.

We held our hands locked for a long time, until long after the heartbeat at the end of my finger weakened.

# Five ❧

𝒜T DUSK I walked down to the swinging bridge where the air felt cooler than any place else, and I sat down, letting my legs dangle. Cold air and colder spray sprang up from the creek. Pinching the week-old but still rosy cut on my fingertip until it smarted, I thought about childbirth—about Isidore, who had been laboring in the town hospital since early morning, about blood swirling against a porcelain tub. How Momma had gone through the same broken water, blood, and childbirth pains, and so had Grandma Lyons, and her mother before her: hundreds of mothers back to some mastodonic cave. *Blood, thicker than water.* I remembered the searchers moving like ghosts across our yard and the three-noted song piped into the dusk.

Once, gone to fetch an afghan from Isidore's bed-room, I saw a glass box with baby jewelry. Bracelets and a ring and spoons lay pressed against a satin pillow. Momma was talking with Isidore in the next room, and I lifted the narrow lid, touching the silver very lightly. My heart beat hard, even though I knew that Isidore would show me the jewelry if I dared to ask. I opened a silver locket and found a strand of fine hair, rolled into a hoop and tied with a pink thread. There were a few other things. A tiny I.D. wristband from the hospital. A rib-bon. A birthday candle, broken in half.

My damp hands left prints on the glass lid.

Massey's bridge rocked, squeaking above the noise of water churned to foam against the rocks. Down-stream the black pools stirred, alive with the push of current. I felt sleepy, peaceful on the bridge. Momma would call me if there was any news about Isidore's baby.

As the air under the trees darkened to blue, a boy came down the ridge path, carrying a green bamboo pole and a may-apple leaf packed with dirt and worms. The metal slats felt cool to me after the hot day, and his bare feet made the bridge vibrate, made me shiver. The little boy broke the ribbon of grass tied around his may-apple package, unfolding the leaf. I nodded at him when he knelt down, even though Mr. Massey says there's only one allowed on the bridge at a time. I figured the two of us together weighed less than Mr. Massey all by himself.

*

Second babies move fast, Momma told me, but that didn't prove true for Isidore. Labor lasted all day and into the night before she became a mother again. I was with Isidore in the house on the ridge when her labor started.

"This is it," she said, throwing back the sheet and coverlet.

Awake and up in an instant, I checked the clock—5:01 in the morning—and recorded the time the way Momma had told me to do. I was ready, though I hadn't thought the baby would arrive while I was staying over, with Bill Simms away on night shift. Suddenly I saw that water drenched Isidore's side of the bed.

"Run get towels," she said, pulling the soaked gown away from her legs.

Then while I knelt, rubbing down the bedroom floor, I heard noise—a hiss and sputter—and the shower burst on.

"What are you doing?" I shouted, racing down the hall.

The bathroom was already foggy, Isidore's face wreathed in clouds. The gown still clung to her legs and hips.

She laughed at me. Me! When I, the sensible one, knew what to do. What Momma had told me to do.

"How can you laugh?"

"It's just beginning, Meg. Don't worry—by the time the pushing starts I'll feel quite sure that I'll never laugh again."

Isidore said the nurses might not let her shower and wash her hair, not for days if she had surgery, so she was going to get clean now. Right now. I remembered what Momma said about second babies being faster than first ones. All I could think about was what would I do if the baby simply fell out—a baby all dripping from his ocean and still roped to his mother's body. I ran to the phone, checking names off Isidore's list, my hand shaking.

Dr. Cannon first. My mother once sweet-talked six plank-bottom chairs for the historical society out of him, and he knew me. I told him that Isidore's water had broken. He asked me whether there was any blood. He sounded sleepy. Blood? I repeated. I hadn't thought about the possibility of blood.

"Is there any blood?" I yelled, poking my head in the steamy bathroom.

"Some blood and a little mucus," she called back.

Dr. Cannon did not show what I thought was sufficient alarm. He said for Isidore to come over to the hospital. He'd be there. Later.

Called Momma.

"It's time," I said. Momma did not seem overly alert. "She's washing her hair," I said, emphasizing the *hair*.

"That's good," she said sleepily. "I'm on my way."

"What'll I do if it comes," I said, my voice rising.

"Just use clean scissors," she advised, yawning into the phone.

"Scissors? That's disgusting."

"Just kidding, Meg, sorry. It probably won't come yet," she added. "I'm up, I'm dressing. I'll be there."

"Maybe you'd better hurry," I said. "There's a little blood."

"She's having a baby," Momma informed me, as if I might be in doubt. "It's okay, there's going to be some blood."

Then I rang up Bill Simms. He didn't appear worried either, but at least he and the woman who answered the phone sounded awake and excited.

I hung up and dashed back to the bathroom.

"Are you having any contractions?" I asked, holding my pad and pencil, very businesslike, not even paying attention to Isidore as she started to dry her hair. A thing which normally would have made me feel pretty strange, being in the same room with a towel-clad and very pregnant woman. Stretched like a balloon with too much air, too little skin.

"Sure," she said. "I had some in the shower."

"Some in the shower," I repeated, looking at my pad, 5:01 penciled neatly at the top.

By the time we reached the hospital, Isidore was breathing slowly and deeply, as I imagined a Buddhist monk might breathe just before levitation.

"I'm trying to be somewhere else," she whispered. "Anywhere," she added.

I sat out in the hall while Momma handed her over to some nurses. She said they cheered right up when Isidore came in. They hadn't had a baby in days. *They're* not having one now, I pointed out. While I was waiting, Bill Simms whizzed by.

Then our part was finished, though Momma and I were still keyed up, with no place to go. We did eat breakfast out, but the food wasn't very good.

Back home, Momma sat down with a big block of a history book, and I sat on the front porch steps, listening for the phone. There's a good bit of small activity in the average front yard. When the sun blistered the porch, I dragged myself to the hammock. In the afternoon Fred Massey dropped by. We stretched out side-by-side in the big hammock, sweating, not quite touching. I felt as though my hormones had died; as though I might not ever want to be kissed again. Staring into the fir tree, I tried to remember the worst stomachache of my life.

"It makes you think," I murmured.

Fred was so close that I could see sweat pooling in the

pores of his nose. On his ears stood small tufts of hair like the big tufts on Mr. Massey's ears. It occurred to me that he wasn't perfect, that his children could have fine tufts on their ears.

The day droned on, terribly hot.

*

At visiting hours the next day I should have backed politely out of the room since Isidore was obviously asleep. But from outside the ceiling-to-floor hospital curtains no one could tell that I watched—that I always watched Isidore when I could, as if I could learn a secret from her face. At rest she had a sad look, the corners of her mouth turned faintly downward, her skin pulled a little too tightly across her temples.

When I stared at her, I couldn't help remembering what had happened to me. Couldn't help imagining white limbs rolling in the black water. Isidore, so dark and pale, could remind me without a word.

As I stood inside the curtains, gripping a bunch of violets I had picked in the woods earlier that morning, I saw again that Isidore was beautiful. No room remained for anything but her beauty and her sadness and a dark sense of change, of events not fully seen, not known— like catching that glimpse of whiteness sliding under the water. The instant was gone; Isidore's eyes opened and I smiled at her. A part of me realized, without the least surprise, that I loved Isidore.

Who knows why I began to love Isidore so that she became a sort of icon to me? Even then I knew that Little Jordan was at the beginning of it—the dead child that I held in my arms and the image of Isidore, bowed down in the green dusk.

*

"Milk from the moon, Zander," I said, the bottle of Isidore's milk cool in my hand.

Alexander and I sat under the tallest of tall walnut trees. Only fine limp grass would grow under the walnut trees, whose leaves threshed the sunlight out and away. Even in late July the shadows could hold pockets of moist and chill air. I shifted in a wire chair, trying not to listen to the distant rise and fall of Momma arguing with Len Jarrett. They were occupying the house, so

Zander and I retreated to the trees.

The baby's eyes fastened to mine. I smiled at him, although it really made me feel funny when he looked up—I had seen how he stared and stared into Isidore's eyes when he drank from her breasts. And there was something uncanny about the whole idea. Zander feeding off Isidore. First Zander inside her, then outside but still connected, then growing up and not remembering a thing about it.

*Zander* was my name for Isidore's baby. Alexander seemed too big a name for a baby to carry around. Momma called him Alexander for a week, until she shortened it to Alex. Half the time she called him Zander too, though.

We kept the baby for half an hour or so almost every day, morning or afternoon, depending on when Bill Simms worked. He wanted Isidore to go out more. He and Momma talked about the post-partum blues. Myself, I didn't think Isidore depressed.

Once she confessed that she was glad the baby was a boy.

"I might have gotten mixed up," she said.

I think she told me because she knew I wouldn't tell anyone. Not even Momma. That one time remained the only time she ever said a word about her daughter after Zander was born. Not that Isidore mentioned her by name. I never said the name either. Just Zander's.

I hadn't taken a real hard look at a baby before, although I noticed that some of the ones I saw people adoring appeared fairly homely. Not Zander. He was simply beautiful, very rosy and peaceful with slate-colored eyes that verged on black. Some days his long hair stuck up in spikes, and then he took on a comic look.

It seemed strange to me that babies emerged from nowhere, or almost nowhere, and suddenly they were very firmly and fiercely here and their mothers utterly mad about them.

So. I sat quietly at Momma's ice-cream-parlor table with Zander, trying to burp him, and thinking some very serious thoughts like where babies come from and why and whether I could ever be crazy about a cute baby like Zander. Whether the whole mystery of babies had anything to do with God. What Fred Massey would look like when he was forty. Stuff like that. Momma always says that teenagers are made to think more than anyone else. That means I was just sitting there at the ice cream table, innocently doing my job in life.

To make events absolutely clear, Zander and I had nothing to do with what happened. Which was that Len blew through the door like something spat out. Steamed past me and Zander without so much as a grunt of disgust. Vanished fast as a spell at the corner of the yard. I heard his car start; red veils of dust floated up from the dirt road.

I looked over my shoulder. Bumping his cheek against mine, Zander looked too.

Momma lounged in the doorway. I glanced away. I didn't want her to know that I had been watching. In a minute she came up behind me and stroked Zander's hair. His poor little head bobbled up and down.

"Well, that's settled," she said.

I waited a moment.

"Well, what's settled," I said. Zander collapsed against my chest, letting out a shriek and pulling his legs up.

"Another man down the drain," she said.

I patted the baby, up and down his back the way Momma had shown me. Already I felt like an expert. My hand beat a tune on his spine, a happy rhythm.

"Too bad," I said.

"I haven't entirely given him up," she said.

I rubbed Zander's back. He was huddled into a ball. He looked a bit like a turtle.

"But I will," she said after a minute.

Zander stretched his limbs convulsively and burped. Loudly.

"Let me take that baby," Momma said. Startled by her grasp, Zander seemed to swim up, his eyes round and his outstretched arms paddling the air.

I stared at the ground. I was caught off guard—surprised to find that I felt sorry. Not sorry that another Mr. Wrong was disappearing from our lives. Just sorry. Momma's fan-shaped feet looked pitiful and unprotected in the thin grass. Tears jumped to my eyes and I rubbed Zander's burp cloth across my face.

"Don't do that," Momma said.

"Momma," I said, "why don't you ever wear shoes?"

Zander let loose a small, pert yell. Momma didn't

answer, for there was Isidore, just then entering our yard and starting to run toward us.

*

"One more day of July," Momma said. "Then August. We'll be with Grandma and Grandpa."

We would stay away for two whole weeks, and Fred Massey was going to write me a letter.

"Then school," Momma said. "No more afternoons under the wisteria."

"No more listening to the creek."

Momma glanced at me but didn't answer.

It was our last visit to the Simmses' house before we left for the shore; Isidore had fallen asleep on the porch swing, her head thrown to one side. Perspiration soaked the curls near her face, made pinpricks above her lip.

Leaning forward, Momma rocked Zander's cradle. Mosquito netting billowed over him and spilled to the floor. The clouds of mesh lent him a romantic, faraway look. His arms and legs pedaled, as though he was dreaming of motion.

"There's Len." Momma stood up abruptly. He carried

a stick, slashing at the meadow grass, lopping off seed heads and flowers. Momma followed him with her eyes a long time before she walked to the edge of the street and waved.

"No," I could hear her saying. "Maybe after Meg and I are home from the beach."

She turned back to the porch.

"Come on, Meg; let's go."

"But Isidore's asleep," I said. "What about Zander?"

"They'll be fine. Bill should be home any minute."

Len didn't even glance at me, just began hurrying Momma along the meadow path. She kept turning back, gesturing for me to come with them. When they gained the ridge, she drew away from him.

"Meg," she called.

So I followed.

Arms folded, Len lounged against a tree. Momma made me walk with them, but at the swinging bridge Len tugged her close. There was barely room for two.

Momma pulled away from him. I couldn't hear what she said over the stream's noise. I don't believe she was informing him that Mr. Massey allows only one at a time on the bridge.

"Momma," I shouted. "I'm going back to Isidore's. I'll be home later." By that time Len and Momma might have finished their argument, although it looked to be a good one.

I flew back up the bank, up from the cool streaming air of the creek. When I paused, I could hear Momma calling my name, and I hesitated a moment before I broke and fled out of the trees and into the meadow, toward the white house and the wisteria porch where, when Isidore woke, I could say anything.

*

An hour later I was home and hungry, sorry that I hadn't stayed for dinner with Isidore and Bill. With one foot I rocked myself idly, pushing against the soft ground under the hammock, so that dirt puffed into the air. Whenever I stopped, the heat thickened around me, my arms and legs growing heavy as Little Jordan stone. Momma and Len's angry talk grew faint, fainter; they shrank to tiny bees, tickling my ear with their buzzing.

"Wake up, Meg, wake up."

It was night when Momma shook me awake and I

stumbled into the house. I lay down on Momma's bed, hugging a pillow.

"When we get back," she told me, "it'll be just you and me. Just the two of us rambling around together."

She sank down on the very edge of the mattress.

"I must have been crazy to stay with Len as long as I did. Maybe I won't go out with another man until you're grown and gone away to college."

I turned my face to the wall, sleepy but certain that Momma's personal history was doomed to repeat itself.

"Did you eat with Isidore and Bill?"

When I shook my head, Momma sighed and got back up.

"I'm sorry Meg," she said.

"It's okay."

"No, it's not—I'm going to make you a sandwich right now."

"Momma."

"What?"

"I've been thinking. Not because of anything in particular—I guess Hinton isn't really that bad."

"Yes," Momma said. "I've always said so."

I settled into sleep, falling deeper by degrees, the clattering of Momma moving about in the kitchen fading away gradually. She must have come back with plate in hand, only to find me sprawled across the bed, eyes shut. Floating in sleep, I dreamed that Len Jarrett banged with a rock on our front door. The stone struck with a terrible, hollow sound. I heard Momma's feet fly down the hall, making a light slapping, but she took her time to answer. I dreamed low, murmuring voices, and then I stood at a window, looking down, holding Momma's pillow in my arms.

*He's nothing but a poor, dead man, fished from the brook,* I heard someone say.

Soaked, speckled with leaf litter, Len was weeping, though I can hardly believe that Len Jarrett would cry, even in my dreams. He knelt down by Momma's bare feet, and though she spoke angrily and waved him away, he would not go. I couldn't find heart to hate him any longer, leaning my head against the windowpane to watch until I grew weary of his stream of tears and dreamed only of sleep.

I never told anyone but Isidore about the sound of

that stone pounding against wood in the night.

She was quiet, thinking about Momma.

"That was no dream," she said. "Ellen has a loving, forgiving nature. She would go to the door."

"But Len," I asked, not expecting any answer but my own, "could Len Jarrett cry?"

# *Six* ৵

I**T WASN'T** because the land and sea and even moonlight were scaled with shine, like fish, but there was a look about the place that made summers at the beach house the same, long summer. Not that the district appeared changeless. Every year Momma pointed out that the town had cast its moorings nearer to Grandma and Grandpa's cottage, lodged in the sunlit curve of the national seashore. It seemed to us that the path from the house through the low scrub and sea oats grew more distinct. But the light stayed the same light, and the breeze lapping our backs and the cool dark inside the cottage on its low stilts were the same. Inside hung watercolors Grandma had painted when she was a girl: blanket flowers and gaudy nameless beach blossoms which looked nothing like our mountain flowers. On most days the air inside seemed suspended, and no breeze from outside ever sapped its well-like coolness or blew away its shadows.

So when I raced up the sand yard to the house, as I did every year, to surprise Grandma and Grandpa Lyons, I forgot everything that had gone before and was caught up in the hours of childhood. My grandma met me on the bleached, silvery porch, and I loved her more than ever, even though earlier I had thought maybe I was getting so grown-up that a grandmother might not mean as much. Because in between visits you forget how she smells of lilacs and how soft her skin is, forget how an old person is really just as interesting as anybody else, maybe more so if we're talking about my grandparents. Grandpa came out of their bedroom, his shirt crumpled, and when he hugged me he held me delicately and a long time, the way I've seen him hold an injured bird. I hugged him back, ducking my head against his chest so no one could see my wet eyes. Thinking didn't have anything to do with that grief, but if it had, it would have been about how Momma had told me Grandpa Lyons was sick; yet that had not meant much to me except in twinges now and then during the past seven months.

Being far and away makes a person forget; what's important can't be seen across a distance. I learned about distance and about seeing at close range that summer. I believed what I touched with my hands. That summer I was busy running up against things, learning what they meant.

\*

The first hour of the day I owed to Grandpa. And all my weeks at the beach blended into one week, one day. Always, the fresh air rushed at us, the sun blazed on us and waves and crumbs of quartz in the sand. Always, the nights snapped shut like a fan to be shaken open in morning's blare of light. Floating voices and lamplight swayed on the water all night. For thirteen summers I had dropped into sleep like someone stumbling and falling, swift and clean into dark water with no snakes, no touching bottom.

At dawn Grandpa and I scouted the shore, taking note of the light but not talking about it, just letting it rest on our shoulder blades, something big and unspoken between us. The belt of sand from sea oats to sea was spare and simple except when we neared the village. Then we might discover fish heads in a scribble of line or a picket row of blackened sparklers.

The walk had become a tradition with us. When I was three or four Grandpa carried me on his shoulders, lunging and roaring into the sea wind. I remember the feel of his thick hair bunched in my fists—coarse and clean-smelling as sea grass. In those days we would scream, jolt across the sand; when I was thirteen, we often stopped to rest. Everything else kept booming along under the wind and water. The wind blew Grandpa's thick white hair one way, then another.

The first time we stopped, Grandpa dozed on his side in the sand. He held so still and quiet that I touched him to make sure he was okay. He didn't open his eyes. After a minute he placed his hand on my arm.

"You've had a big summer," he said. I had to inch closer to hear him.

"Yes." I laced my fingers with his. They were long and slender, dried by the wind and sun.

"Little Meg," he whispered.

"That's what Bill Simms calls me." I rolled over on my stomach so I could watch Grandpa's face. When my shadow touched him, his eyes opened.

"Simms. Your pretty neighbor."

"Isidore."

"That's right. Ellen told us, but I forgot the name." Grandpa closed his eyes again.

"She's very beautiful and sad. Then of course there's Zander, the baby."

"You did a brave thing," Grandpa said.

The sand was dotted with bleached fragments of turrets, conchs, and jingles. I combed my hands across the surface, looking for a perfect shell. Now I knew what Grandpa meant by a big summer.

"I don't know." I poured sand back and forth from one hand to the other. "I was scared."

"When I was a boy, we always touched the dead. Washed them—that was a woman's task—and kissed them good-bye. You didn't grow up without death." Grandpa shielded his eyes and looked past me at the sea, at combers and the swelling beyond the combers and the blurred place where the sea vanished. "Today it's taboo. We're all terrified by a corpse."

I thought about how Isidore had wanted to cradle her little girl's body before burial.

"I'm not," I said. "Not much. Not any more." Leaning down, kissing my grandfather's dead face, mussing the white hair—that was something I could imagine, could do.

"Your grandmother says we'll wake together on the Last Day."

"What do you think?" I asked.

"I don't know. After a century, what's left to raise but strands of hair and dust?"

"Don't ask Momma," I said. "That's the way she talks. I don't know anything about anything—she never tells me about God, even though it's history, isn't it?—and last year in school I asked who Jonah was and everybody laughed at me. But I'm going to find out for myself."

"That's good," Grandpa said, smiling, his eyes drawn back to the sea.

"I like Grandma's ideas better, though. Besides, Fred

Massey told me the very same thing," I said.

Grandpa laughed.

"Fred Massey? I remember Fred Massey. A little mop top with nothing on but a white t-shirt. His mother tearing after him. A plump, red-faced woman."

"Well, he keeps his pants on now," I said. My face flushed, the color rising in my cheeks until they must have been as red as Mrs. Massey's.

Grandpa sat up cross-legged in the sand and looked at me, very seriously. His eyes were crinkled up at the corners.

"You're a good girl, Meg," he said.

\*

On our third night at the beach the moaning of the sea woke me. I got out of bed, surprised and a little frightened. Nights at the beach felt seamless, almost didn't exist. Once Isidore told me that a baby believes that the world stops when he sleeps. That's how I lived at the beach. To be awake and moving in the dark: something was awry.

A sea breeze was running through the shadowy front

rooms. The moonlight outside burnished the grass and creeks; I could see miles of marshland. The light looked as though it had been tilted from a cup, flooding the ground.

In the kitchen I drank thirstily. The light from the old, round-topped refrigerator leaked into the room. Setting my glass down in the sink, I stared out the kitchen windows. Manes of marsh grass thrashed back and forth. The wind blew the hair back from my face and cooled my damp neck.

I padded through the front rooms. Light glowed on the floor below the windows and the door, which stood open to the moon and wind. Sliding the screen open, I stood in the wash of moonlight. It must be early, I thought, but whether early in the night or in the morning, I could not tell. I leaned on the porch rail, letting the wind sweep around me, gazing over the creeks and scrub at each side.

Just before dark I had glimpsed a bird climbing the wind as if it were a staircase. That's how the windy dark felt: as though I could mount up and up into the sky.

My nightgown whipped against me when I stepped

down to the patch of cleared yard. I walked along the edge of the house but stopped, startled. Grandma and Momma—one seated, one standing—were under the porch cupola.

Momma had unplaited the braids that hung down my grandma's back at night, and now she combed the long rippling hair. It made a cape on Grandma's shoulders, seemed to splash past her feet.

They were talking, but I couldn't hear a word. Grandma spread her hands out in a gesture of helplessness. Momma kept on with the comb. For a long time I watched, leaning on the white trellis that Grandpa had built, holding on to the latticework and the Morning Glory vines. At night the spent blooms puckered into rags; for them, there really was nothing but day. The night didn't exist; we didn't exist. We were less than dreams.

I climbed back up the stairs. The house had become a shell, echoing the noise of the sea and wind. But a shell only sings you the whispering sound of your own blood, and this was a bigger sound than my heart and blood. I followed the moaning, tolling noise until I came to a room where the sea surged and cried behind a door. When I touched the knob, the door flew open, the sea wind unwinding before me.

"Grandpa," I called.

Waterfalls of sheets and summer blankets tumbled from the bed, a vortex of salt air rumpling linens, my grandpa's hair, a cast-off robe. The sound ruled over everything.

"Grandpa."

I shook him by the shoulders. He didn't wake. I shook him harder. One bright slit of eye winked shut.

"Wake up, Grandpa."

His eyelids fluttered.

"Are you okay, Grandpa? Should I fetch you anything?"

I put my face close to his so I could hear the words.

"Meg."

"I'm here," I said. "I heard you and I'm here."

"Don't go," he said. "I'm all right but don't go yet."

"I won't, Grandpa. Do you want anything?"

"No. Yes. Maybe you could shut out the wind." His hands trembled on the sheets.

The windows were heavy, glass thrumming in the sash, wood stuck to wood by salty moisture. One and then the other crashed to its sill. I heaved the bedroom door closed. Now the wind flowed smoothly under the door, now a thread of air spiraled through a crack in a window.

I piled the covers back on the bed, tucking in the corners of the sheets.

Grandpa drowsed off again, snoring with his mouth open.

"Grandpa," I sang, "Grandpa."

I stroked his hair in the dark. The moaning kept up, pealing lower and then louder again. How long did I stroke his hair? I wondered whether the moon had risen or sunk.

I crept into the bed and curled around Grandpa's back, latching on to his mane of hair and the cocoon of sheets around his body.

The sound of the sea loomed over the house like a wave. I was singing louder, calling his name. A wave struck the house, and my mouth echoed its thunder. When the wave withdrew, sinking and grating against shells and pebbles, it pulled us into its ocean of sound.

All night we slept buried in its caverns.

*

Each day of our visit my grandpa napped for most of the afternoon. Momma stayed with him so Grandma could get out of the house. Usually she had errands to do, but a few times we hiked along the shore, my grandma striding briskly. Once we spent an afternoon floating on the tidal creeks.

Grandma's canoe was slender and light, and she could lift and carry it over her head. She was pleased with the boat's sleekness and the pale strips of wood fused so closely together that there were no gaps, no unevenness.

When she bent over and let it drop to the water, the canoe landed like a leaf, slapping the water with barely a sound or splash. Insect songs, a high, serrated racket, rose from the marsh and the brackish creeks we navigated. Sometimes I glimpsed claws twiddling up toward the surface and backing down again. Scrubby, nameless trees crouched over the water. Grandma hacked down any ungainly limbs, keeping the water open so she could paddle freely up and down the meandering creeks and branching dead-end rivulets.

"There's a night heron."

She pulled her paddle out of the water and let the canoe drift.

The bird, balanced on one leg, eyed the shallows; then, jabbing past the surface, the heron snatched a silver fish and withdrew into the grasses and shadows.

Grandma sighed.

"You'd think the world would stop being so interesting." She looked at me and smiled. "I'm afraid the beach isn't turning out to be as pleasant as usual this year."

"I'm glad we came," I said. And I was glad too, glad to be with my grandparents and to make Grandpa Lyons laugh, to get a letter from Fred and a card from Isidore.

Grandma dipped her oar back in the water.

"Good."

I remembered what I had seen on the porch. Today Grandma's braids were coiled in a neat wheel at the nape of her neck.

"When you let down your hair—" I hesitated.

Grandma thrust the canoe off a snag.

"How long is it?" I asked.

"Why did you think of that? I don't know. Long. Not

so long as it used to be. Old people droop and change. Noses get bigger, ears and feet too. Hair, hair thins and breaks."

"You must have had an awful lot of hair when you were young," I said.

"Yes, I did. Everyone said thick hair was a woman's great beauty, but I hardly knew what to do with it all."

Grandma stared down the curved banks.

"Your grandpa wouldn't let me cut my hair. He said it mimicked the weather at sea—so changing, so plentiful. My hair was light chestnut, about the color of yours. He could see colors in it, strands of red and gold and flax. Sometimes I thought he married me so he could undo my hair."

I had a sudden vivid picture of Grandma like Eve in an oil painting, a young and pretty Eve with scads of silvery hair. Only of course it wouldn't be silver. It would be a color like mine. It would sweep over her bare shoulders, splashing past her feet. My Grandpa, with his young man's hands, would be weaving his fingers through her hair, unplaiting and combing out her braids.

Somewhere beyond the frame where they played as

lovers and Grandpa combed my Grandma's hair, Momma would be snoozing, a baby, her mouth open like a bird's. I lay there too, half of me, an infinitely small egg sleeping in my child-Momma's body.

Now here was my grandma, talking to me as though I were a grown woman.

"At night he combed my hair until it untangled and the brush sank through easily, as through water. He said that to lie in bed with my hair was like sleeping on the waves."

She paused.

"That was a sweet time in my life."

Grandma laid the paddle across the canoe. She leaned toward me, over the bar between us.

"You have my hair, not your mother's. She was a pretty, fair child. But you have the hair of my mother and grandmother before me. You should let it grow, Meg. Long hair gives a person strength."

She laughed.

"Well," she said, "that's what my grandmother used to say."

\*

*August 9*
*Dear Fred,*

*I bet you wish you were down here baling sea oats instead of hay. I am having a good time, though we didn't get to go deep sea fishing after all. My grandpa doesn't feel well enough to go. We crab, though, just about every day.*

*I swam past the breakers with some kids from town. We dog-paddled out to where the water tilts back and forth only a little bit. Something big brushed against me. I thought it might be a whale. Then I thought maybe it was a shark! Coming back in, I felt too tired to swim, and the gravel cut up my legs. Grandma was worried, and Momma got really mad. She made me promise that you and I wouldn't jump off the dam. Not that the reservoir has anything to do with the ocean. (No snakes!) I said we wouldn't go again this summer.*

*My grandpa remembers when you were a tiny boy. He said some funny things about you.*

*Love,*
*Meg*

*

My grandma quit painting when she married. She said her talent was too small. Maybe, maybe not, I can't say. She kept up sketching, drawing me or Momma when we came for visits, marsh plants and sea creatures, people on the beach.

Even if she gave up paint, she still made things. She loved to follow the "creek walks," her trimmed canoe trails. Then there were "marsh walks." Long before my birth, before they began living year-round at Balish, she and Grandpa built narrow, crooked boardwalks in the marsh. Every year the walks had to be repaired and shored up. In the evenings we relaxed on the boardwalk or the deck, sheltered under one of Grandma's giant canvas parasols. When insects wavered up from the marsh, she draped curtains of mosquito netting over the canvas and lit citronella candles. Balish looked like a festival place, a big yellow moon tugging itself free from the waves, candles floating across the creek on small, makeshift rafts. Their hearts of fire flickered inside paper sacks, plain or pierced or colored with symbols that each meant something to my grandmother.

"Water lights," she called them.

"There is something about making a lantern for a candle," she said. "Something special. Secret."

That summer I decorated a lantern, blue in places for Little Jordan's tumble to the sea, white for mystery, with a rough part all slit and colored green and dull gold for the marsh grass around Balish. My candle sulked and wouldn't burn well. It hung up on the pilings until I knocked the raft away with a stick. Finally the light flamed clear and the sack wobbled off, stopping and starting at the stream's margin.

My candle was a remembrance of Isidore's child; it drifted, burning on water spilled by far-off mountain streams. I was beginning to understand my grandma better, beginning to understand what Fred Massey meant about church candles and why someone sailed flowers on Little Jordan.

"Grandma, how could you give up painting?" I had asked her.

"I chose to stop—I didn't have the singleness of heart to paint. To say, this is what I am, what I must do, and to give up so much else."

She waved her hand toward Momma, sitting with Grandpa under an umbrella.

"Your whole life is a making—trying to build Eden, like a magpie, out of trash and glitter. After all, we were made and so can't help wanting to make things in return."

She put her arm around my shoulders and hugged me.

"Everything's waiting for you, Meg. Maybe you'll have it—that devotion."

"But I can't paint, Grandma."

"You'll see," she said. "There'll be something for you."

I dangled my feet off the boardwalk and the minnows nibbled my toes. My grandma leaned back on the warm boards, closing her eyes.

"There'll be something," she promised.

*

*August 11*
*Dear Hinton,*

*Here I am on the south porch at Balish. I guess you probably sat right where I'm sitting, back when you used to come visit.*

*I have been thinking about what I will do. I haven't decided on much yet except to let my hair grow, but I'm thinking about the other stuff.*

*If you like, I will meet you at Grandma Hinton's for a weekend next summer. I haven't seen her in several years. Don't concern yourself if that isn't what you want to do. It won't hurt my feelings or bother me. This is just if you come back for a visit and if you would like to get together.*

*Hello to your daughter, if that is appropriate.*


*Sincerely,*
*Meg*

\*

"It's hard to think of the beach without Grandpa."

"Yes," Momma said, "it is very hard."

Grandma had set me to imagining the future again. My hair would grow to be like hers when she was a girl, but Grandpa wouldn't be there to see. Hinton might see it, but to him I would never be a girl with beautiful chestnut hair.

The hardest letter I wrote that summer was the one I wrote to Hinton. I really didn't want to see him be-cause it had been too long and I didn't feel any affection for him. I knew he could hurt me—wound me in small ways that I would later remember at odd moments. Then why did I write him that stiff, uncomfortable letter? I don't know. Because a father is a father? And at least an idea to be honored? Because what's important needs to be touched, to be seen up close? Maybe I wrote it because I held the memory of a dead child in my arms, because Grandpa would die no matter what I did or thought or whether I prayed or not. Because we die, even Hinton, my careless father.

In the evenings when I watched the moon swim up

out of the sea, my eyes were wet. I wanted her to stay the same, a round, unbitten apricot glowing on an invisible branch. But each night brought us a different moon.

# Seven ᢙ

"Sorry. Did I startle you?" Momma's hand grazed my hair. "I thought we might go for a walk, just you and me."

"You know I can't, Momma; you know I promised Fred." Lifting up the hem of my dress, I waded along the banks of Little Jordan.

The night wind had swept the sky clear of all but a stray cloud and the morning's moon that floated over the blue mountains like a pale watermark. Momma and I sat down and shared a big steppingstone for a while. When she wandered back to the house, I felt bad, as if it were my fault she had forgotten.

I was going to church with Fred Massey. Later, I intended to look hard at the boy-child who gripped symbols of a spinning world and its people like toys—a top, a dollhouse—in his hands. I wanted to look at his mother, the Madonna. When I tried to call back her image, I saw Isidore with twilight like a robe on her shoulders, holding Zander in her lap. And I wanted to find Isidore's daughter in the cemetery behind the picket fence, to feel her stone-cut name with my hand. I meant to examine all of it, from the men and women in robes ironed by Mrs. Massey to the altar to the red cushions tucked under the pews.

"I'll find You out if I can," I whispered into the stream.

Water teases away everything, even thoughts, sails them east of the mountains and plains to the sea. Seated on a chill stepping-stone of Little Jordan, I remembered the salt rivulets around Balish. Already the berries and flowers of late summer would be changing on the creeks. As the months passed and Indian summer came and then fell away, the moon and sea and tidal marshes would turn bare and lovely, while Grandpa Lyons dwindled in his big snowy bed. Maybe in the end he would dream of my grandma's beautiful hair, as tumbling and alive as water. It might be strong enough to bear him up.

*

"It's not that simple, is it?" I asked the stream.

Surely no one would say that a child sinking into a pool of Little Jordan was necessary. Still, Isidore's child would lie at the back of anything I could do or be. If there was any place in me as pure and deep as the stream pool, it held a child who would never grow up. But I felt so alive—immortal—even with that knowledge. It seemed to me that, in crossing Little Jordan on a certain summer's day, I had begun to see in a wide and clear light.

A rock splashed into the water.

"Fred?"

The wind tipped the minnowy leaves one way, then schooled them back again.

"Fred Massey?" No, not yet. It was still early.

What must have been fall's first red leaf skated by my feet. White and airy as foam, torn flowerheads swirled in pursuit. Who sailed blossoms like boats down Little Jordan was still one of the summer's mysteries.

I stared at them. I knew the very spot where those flowers grew.

Kicking my shoes into the grass, I raced up our dirt

road. My skirts were bunched in my hands, and in a moment I ran for the sheer pleasure of movement, flinging up pebbles and a soft powder that would coat my toes and ankles. There: the glade of Black Cohosh, its tall spires broken. I sprinted on, panting as I neared the one-at-a-time bridge. The stream dived through the rock bed, singing loudly.

I smiled; in the quiet morning air Mr. Massey's pedestrian bridge was swinging.

The cold wire and slats felt good to my bare feet. Chill air surrounded me, floating up past ferns and weeds to the overhanging branches. Holding on, turning slowly in a circle, I scanned the shore and the ridge. Late summer's dragonflies sprang into the air. An arrowhead of bright, empty meadow sparkled between trees.

"I almost caught you, whoever you are," I shouted into the roar of Little Jordan's white water. "Next time I'll find you."

I spun around on Mr. Massey's swinging bridge. When I suddenly held still, the hills reeled under the watermark moon, and the bright arrowhead of meadow danced like a gold top in the leaves.

## NOTE ABOUT THE AUTHOR

MARLY YOUMANS is a poet and fiction writer living in the Chapel Hill area of North Carolina. Her work has previously been published in *Ploughshares, Southern Humanities Review, Black Warrior Review,* and *The Little Magazine.* LITTLE JORDAN is her first book.